Treasure Chest Readers
Stop That Stew!

Text by Margaret Mahy

Illustrations by Deborah Rigby

Published in 2010 by Windmill Books, LLC
303 Park Avenue South, Suite # 1280, New York, NY 10010-3657

Adaptations to North American Edition © 2010 Windmill Books, Copyright © 2008 by Autumn Publishing

Published in 2008 by Autumn Publishing, A division of Bonnier Media Ltd., Chichester, West Sussex, PO20 7EQ, UK

CREDITS: Text by Janine Scott, Illustrations by Deborah Rigby

Library of Congress Cataloging-in-Publication Data

Mahy, Margaret.
 Stop that stew! / Margaret Mahy ; illustrations by Deborah Rigby. -- 1st North American ed.
    p. cm. -- (Treasure chest readers)
 Published in Great Britain in 2008 by Autumn Publishing.
 Summary: On the way in his little red car to share a big pot of stew with his friend, Mr. Winkle is unaware of the long procession forming behind him.
 ISBN 978-1-60754-682-5 (library binding) -- ISBN 978-1-60754-683-2 (pbk.) -- ISBN 978-1-60754-684-9 (6-pack)
 [1. Stews--Fiction. 2. Humorous stories.] I. Rigby, Deborah, ill. II. Title.
 PZ7.M2773St 2010
 [E]--dc22
                                    2009040147

Manufactured in the United States of America

CPSIA Compliance Information: Batch #BW01W: For further information contact Windmill Books, New York, New York at 1-866-478-0556.

alphabet
s o u p™
an imprint of
WINDMILL BOOKS™
New York

One sunny day, Mr. Winkle woke up early. He put on his chef's hat and apron, and began to make a stew in his big brown pot.

Mr. Winkle added a pinch of this and a pinch of that to the pot. He chopped and stirred. The stew bubbled and boiled. Soon it smelled delicious.

"This stew would be better if I shared it," Mr. Winkle said to himself. "I will go to visit my friend Tom and take the stew with me."

Mr. Winkle went out to his tiny red car. He put the big brown pot on the roof of the car while he opened the door. Then he got in the car and drove away.

As Mr. Winkle drove down the lane, two dogs caught a whiff of the stew. They sniffed and sniffed. It smelled wonderful. The two dogs chased the tiny red car.

8

The dog-catcher saw the two dogs chasing Mr. Winkle's car.

"I'd better catch those dogs!" she announced, and she immediately drove off in her dog-catcher's van.

Just then, Mrs. Bright peeked out of the window and saw the dog-catcher following the two dogs. "Those are my dogs!" she cried. "I must tell the dog-catcher."

Mrs. Bright grabbed her helmet and climbed on her scooter. Off she sped, following the dog-catcher, who was following the dogs, who were following the wonderful-smelling stew in the big brown pot on the roof of the tiny red car.

Just then the police were driving by in their police car. "What's going on?" they said. "We'd better find out!"

So the police followed Mrs. Bright, who was following the dog-catcher, who was following the dogs, who were following the wonderful-smelling stew in the big brown pot on the roof of the tiny red car.

As Mr. Winkle neared his friend's house, he suddenly remembered, "Oh no! Today is Friday. Tom is at work! I'd better go home. How sad it is that there is no one to share my wonderful stew."

Mr. Winkle drove all the way home and stopped outside his own house.

The two dogs, the dog-catcher, Mrs. Bright, and the police stopped near the tiny red car. Mr. Winkle was searching for the stew. He looked on the front seat and the back seat, but it wasn't there.

"My delicious stew has disappeared," cried Mr. Winkle.

Everyone pointed and shouted, "Look on the roof of your car, Mr. Winkle!"

"There it is," said Mr. Winkle. "Is anybody hungry?"

"I am!" shouted the dog-catcher.
"I am!" cried Mrs. Bright.
"We are!" agreed the police officers.
"Woof, woof!" barked the two dogs.

"Then come inside and share my delicious stew," said Mr. Winkle. "There is plenty for everyone."

LEARN MORE! READ MORE!

Stop That Stew! is filled with rhythm and repetition—great ingredients for enjoying and improving reading. Here are some more books that use and explore great reading tools like rhyme, rhythm, and repetition.

FICTION
Horowitz, Dave. *Humpty Dumpty Climbs Again.* New York: Putnam Juvenile, 2008.

Seuss, Dr. *Six By Seuss: A Treasury of Dr. Seuss Classics.* New York: Random House, 2007.

NONFICTION
Seuss, Dr. *I'm Not Going to Read Any Words Today: Learn About Rhyming Words.* New York: Random House, 1995.

For more great fiction and nonfiction, go to
www.windmillbooks.com.